Just like you and me

David Miller

DIAL BOOKS FOR YOUNG READERS
NEW YORK

Deep in the jungle
the bird of paradise
loves to show off.

Just like you

and me.

Swiftest of all cats, the golden

cheetah moves like the wind.

Just like you and me!

Gathered in a group,

penguins like to play together.

Just like you

and me.

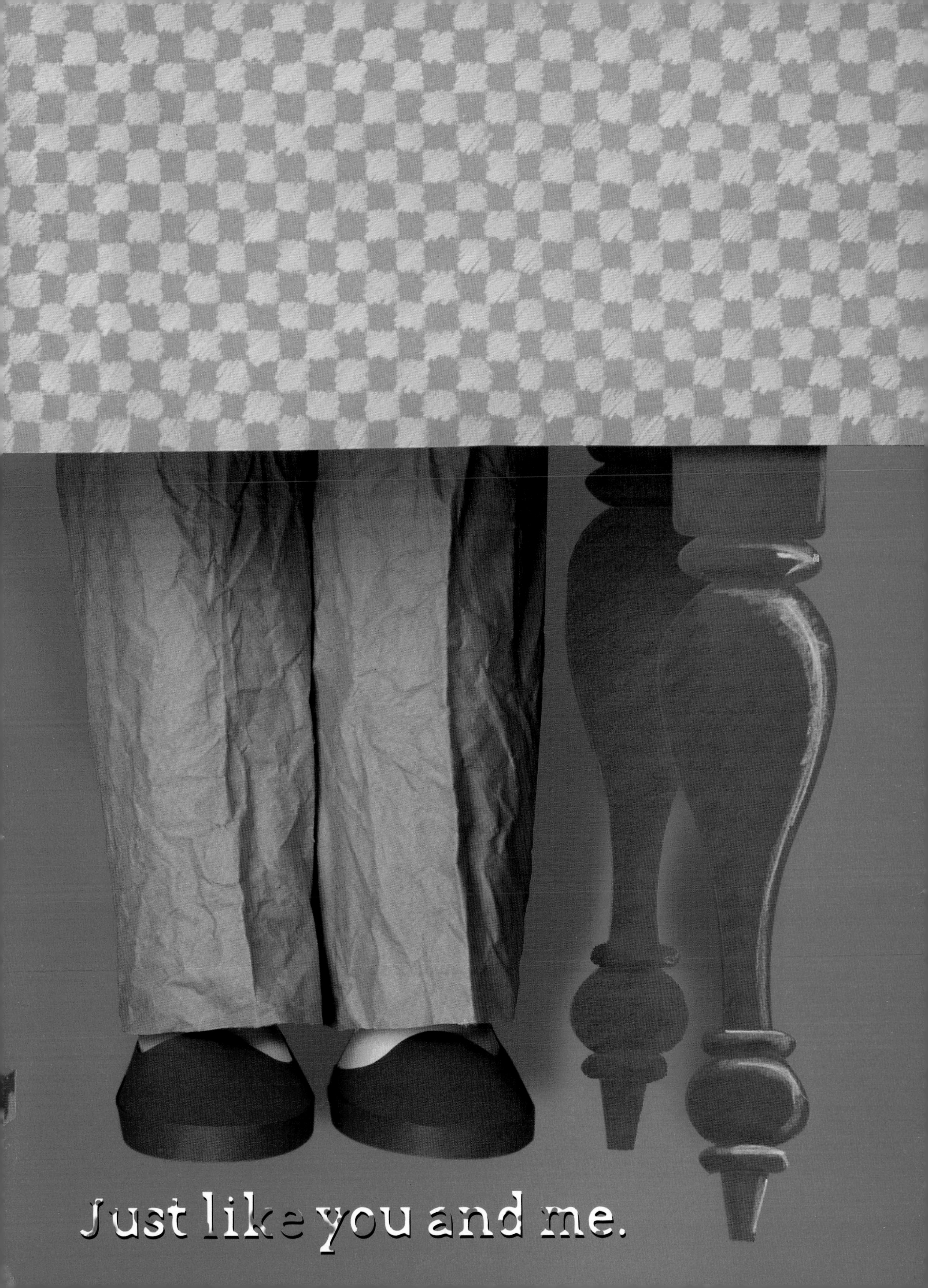

Just like you and me.

On a summer
afternoon,

the noble lion
lounges lazily.

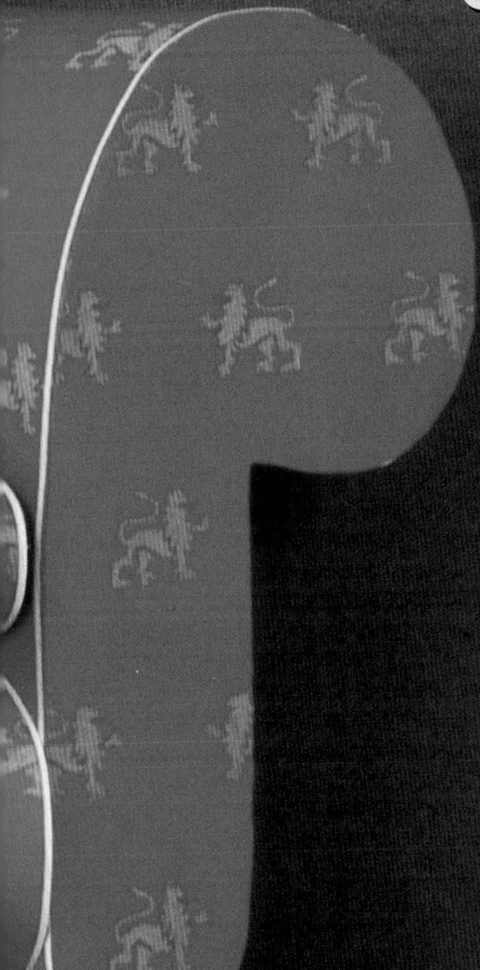

Just like you and me.

Light as drifting smoke,

graceful cranes love to dance.

Just

like

you

and

me.

Protected by their parents,
baby birds are safe and loved.

Just like

you and me!

About the animals

Count Raggi's **bird of paradise** is one of a group of spectacular birds that comes from the forests of New Guinea. The males put on amazing displays with their brilliantly colored feathers to attract the attention of the females.

On the open grassy plains of Africa, the **cheetah** can run at speeds of up to 60 miles per hour to catch its prey. "Cheetah" comes from a Hindi word meaning "spotted one." An adult cheetah weighs 77–143 pounds, stands 28–36 inches tall at the shoulder and is 44-53 inches long (not counting its tail).

In the freezing Antarctic, **penguins** gather in crowds of thousands to mate and rear their young. Penguins are considered to be the most social of birds. As many as 24 million visit the Antarctic each year and they always swim and feed in groups. Their wings, shaped like flippers, help them swim underwater at a speed of up to 25 miles per hour.

The **chameleon** is a tree lizard. Its eyes, set in turrets, can swivel in different directions or focus together in one direction. It catches insects on the sticky end of its tongue (which is as long as its body *and* tail!), shooting it out at 1/25 of a second. A chameleon can also change the color of its skin.

in this book

Lions spend about twenty hours per day relaxing or sleeping. They are the only cats that live in large family groups, called prides. Prides differ in size, but usually consist of two males, seven females, and any number of cubs. In the dark, cool hours of morning the pride's adult females hunt as a team to catch a meal that will be shared by the entire group.

The **crane** is a tall, graceful, long-legged bird that mates for life. Its spectacular courtship dance includes bows, leaps, high steps, and loud trumpeting calls. A crane can sleep perfectly balanced on one leg, with its head tucked under a wing.

The **wedge-tailed eagle** has a wingspan of about 7 feet. It is the largest bird of prey in Australia and can be seen soaring majestically over the countryside. As it flies to great heights, it uses its long, wedge-shaped tail to make quick or awkward turns. Both males and females have black plumage and a dark brown nape, wings, and undertail.

The little **willy wagtail** is a very bold bird that will confront bigger birds, cats, and even snakes. It will flit and dart about catching insects and, when it lands on a post or the back of a grazing animal, will swing its tail back and forth.